The Fiji Flood

A WOODLAND MYSTERY
By Irene Schultz

Wright Group
McGraw-Hill

To my adventurous sister and fellow writer,
Dubby, who first told me about Fiji

The Fiji Flood
Text copyright © Irene Schultz
Illustrations copyright © Wright Group/McGraw-Hill
Cover and cameo illustrations by Taylor Bruce
Interior illustrations by Meredith Yasui
Map illustration by Alicia Kramer

Woodland Mysteries® is a registered trademark of
Wright Group/McGraw-Hill.

Wright Group/McGraw-Hill
19201 120th Avenue NE, Suite 100
Bothell, WA 98011
www.WrightGroup.com

Printed in the United States of America

10 9 8 7

ISBN: 0-7802-7226-9
ISBN: 0-7802-7925-5 (6-pack)

What family solves mysteries...has adventures all over the world...and loves oatmeal cookies?

It's the Woodlanders!

Sammy Westburg (10 years old)
His sister Kathy Westburg (13)
His brother Bill Westburg (14)
His best friend Dave Briggs (16)
His best grown-up friend Mrs. Tandy
And Mop, their little dog!

The children all lost their parents, but with Mrs. Tandy have made their own family.

Why are they called the Woodlanders? Because they live in a big house in the Bluff Lake woods. On Woodland Street!

Together they find fun, mystery, and adventure. What are they up to now?

Read on!

Meet the Woodlanders!

Sammy Westburg

Sammy is a ten-year-old wonder! He's big for his fifth-grade class, and big-mouthed, too. He has wild hair and makes awful spider faces. Even so, you can't help liking him.

Bill Westburg

Bill, fourteen, is friendly and strong, and only one inch taller than his brother Sammy. He loves Sammy, but pokes him to make him be quiet! He's in junior high.

Kathy Westburg

Kathy, thirteen, is small, shy, and smart. She wants to be a doctor some day! She loves to be with Dave, and her brothers kid her about it. She's in junior high, too.

Dave Briggs

Dave, sixteen, is tall and blond. He can't walk, so he uses a wheelchair and drives a special car. He likes coaching high-school sports, solving mysteries, and reading. And Kathy!

Mrs. Tandy

Sometimes the kids call her Mrs. T. She's Becky Tandy, their tall, thin, caring friend. She's always ready for a new adventure, and for making cookies!

Mop

Mop is the family's little tan dog. Sometimes they have to leave him behind with friends. But he'd much rather be running after Sammy.

Table of Contents

Chapter		Page
1	The Bouncing Plane	1
2	The Magician	11
3	Mud Slides!	21
4	An Orange Hug	29
5	Where Will We Sleep?	37
6	The Costume Party	47
7	Mrs. Babberton Turns Purple	57
8	The Water Crew	65
9	The Race with the River	75
10	Stuck!	83
11	Saved!	91
12	Here's the Money!	101
13	The Strangest Animal	111

Chapter 1:
The Bouncing Plane

The huge plane hummed across the sky.

The Woodland family was flying toward the last stop of their trip.

Ten-year-old Sammy Westburg hugged

his swim fins against his chest.

His snorkel tube lay along his cheek ... hanging from a band of rubber around his forehead.

Goggles stuck out of his pocket.

His fourteen-year-old brother Bill handed him a big plastic bag.

He said, "Get a grip, Sammy. Put your snorkeling stuff in here. You might lose something."

Sammy shook his head. "You're just trying to slow me down. I want to go swimming the MINUTE we get near the ocean. ⚡

"I even have my bathing suit on under my jeans. I'm ready for our sunshine vacation!"

Bill laughed. "Then you should wear a skirt like the men on the island do. So you can just slip it off and dive in!"

Sammy said, "I can't wait till we land.

I want to see those guys. Hey, I bet you're kidding me. They don't REALLY wear skirts."

Bill grinned. "Would I kid you? I'm your big brother."

Sammy said, "Sure, but you might just be trying to get even for the rubber worm I put in your bed last night."

Bill said, "Well, this is no trick, Super-pest. In Fiji, lots of men wear skirts!" Bill said the word Fiji like this: FEE-jee.

Their thirteen-year-old sister Kathy leaned forward in her seat. She called softly to them across the aisle, "My ears are stuffed. We must be going in for landing."

Their friend, sixteen-year-old Dave Briggs, was sitting across the aisle from Bill.

He said, "Man, is it stormy out there! I thought the museum letter said the hurricane season would be over on Fiji!"

Mrs. Tandy, the fifth member of the Woodlanders, said, "Someone forgot to tell that to this storm! I hope we can land in all this rain and wind!"

She picked up her knitting to take her mind off the landing. She said, "I bet the Fiji beaches are great."

4

Dave nodded. "I've seen some paintings of South Pacific islands. They're really beautiful. I bet this will be a perfect three days."

Sammy made a face. He said, "I think those paintings look fake."

Dave said, "What do you think looks fake about them?"

Sammy said, "Well, for one thing, all those bright-colored plants. How could a whole island look like that?"

Bill added, "And how about all the pretty girls, with big dark eyes and golden-brown skin?"

Sammy teased, "Sure, you WOULD notice the girls! Bill likes GIRL-els, Bill likes GIR—

"Hey! What's happening!"

The plane shot down like a falling elevator.

Then suddenly it held steady.

Then it headed back up, rolling from side to side.

The loudspeaker boomed, "Attendants, take your seats! Everyone, fasten your seat belts!

Dave said, "The plane's OK, but we must be hitting sudden air changes. That's why we dropped like that."

They couldn't see anything out of the window but big, damp, gray clouds rushing by.

Sammy was scared. He reached for Bill's hand.

He said, "How will the pilot know when we come near land? What if he doesn't see the field in time and we CRASH?"

Bill took Sammy's hand. "It's OK, Sammy. These pilots know how to make blind landings. And anyway, they'll see the field once we get through

these clouds."

But inside Bill was plenty worried.
Mrs. Tandy was knitting double-time, she
was so scared. But she reached over and
patted Sammy's other hand.

Then she took two packages of roasted
peanuts from her knitting bag.

She said, "Here. I saved these for us.
Divide them into five even piles for me,
will you, Sammy?"

Bill said, "And I'll watch to make sure
he counts right."

With something to think about besides

the storm, Sammy felt better.

He had five piles almost ready when ... BANG! Then BOUNCE! Then BAM!

They landed really hard! Oxygen masks came flying down from over-head storage spaces.

The peanuts flew all over the plane.

Somewhere in front a little child began to cry.

But the plane was down safe.

The pilot's voice came over the loudspeaker. "We have landed at Nadi, on Fiji's main island." He said it like this: NON-dee.

"A late storm has taken us by surprise.

"When you get off the plane, run for the building. It's raining cats and dogs!"

The five Woodlanders waited until everyone else got off the plane.

Then Kathy hurried forward and got Dave's wheelchair.

8

Dave swung himself into his chair.

Kathy took Dave down the aisle.

Then, carefully, the four of them helped lower the chair down the steel steps.

They raced toward the airport building.

Rain glued their wet clothes to their bodies.

Water dripped through their hair and down their necks.

Water filled their shoes and socks!

At last they were inside the building ... standing in puddles.

Then Kathy pointed out the big front window and said, "WOW! LOOK AT THAT!"

Chapter 2:
The Magician

For a moment the rain let up.

Kathy was pointing outside to the airport parking lot.

The lot was partly on low ground.

Cars stood in water up to their door handles. One car was in water up to its roof.

Bill said, "Man, I feel sorry for those poor car owners." As he said that, a solid downpour of rain began again.

Just then a tour bus pulled up in front of the building.

Dave saw it and said, "The museum back home planned this trip PERFECTLY. Too bad they couldn't plan the weather!"

The bus looked just the right size for their group of nineteen people ... and all their suitcases.

The bus was red, with a white stripe running from front to back. On the stripe were the words SUNSHINE ISLAND TOURS.

Sammy said, "That should say UNDERWATER TOURS!"

The tour leader, Tina Chow, hurried

the group to the bus, while the Woodlanders waited.

The driver put the suitcases into bins in the side of the bus.

Then Mrs. Tandy said, "Come on! Let's make a dash for it!"

They carried their suitcases out into the heavy rain.

Then they tried to lift Dave aboard, but they were wet and slippery. He almost slid to the ground!

A man already on the bus ran to the front and got off.

It was Glen Taylor, the tallest, skinniest, funniest grown-up in the group.

He said, "Here, let me help!

"You've handled everything so well on this trip, I didn't want to butt in. But this storm is different.

"If you don't mind, I'll stick close ... for as long as this rain lasts."

Dave said, "Thanks! We don't mind at all. We need all the help we can get in this kind of weather!"

They all were aboard now. The driver put away Dave's chair. He locked up the suitcase bins.

Kathy said, "This is a strange beginning for a beach vacation. I hope the storm lets up soon."

Bill looked up at the sky. "I don't think it will, not right away. There's not an inch of blue sky anywhere in sight."

The bus driver came aboard. He turned on the radio.

A voice boomed, "This is a storm alert! Storm waters are washing down from the hills. Drivers, take extra care.

"The sides of some roads have washed away. There is dangerous driving between Nadi and Suva." He said Suva like this: SOO-vuh.

Fiji Island

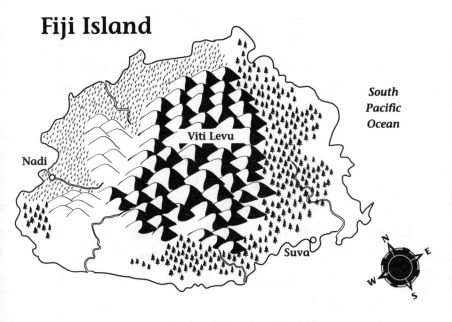

Dave said, "Uh-oh! That's the piece of road we will be on!"

The rain pounded down even harder. Sammy hugged his flippers tighter.

He said, "The rain sounds like a million fingers tapping on top of the bus!"

Bill said, "Look at the windows! It's like being trapped inside a waterfall.

You can hardly see anything!"

Kathy added, "Or how about when you drive your car through a car wash? It's like that, except there isn't anyplace to dry it off."

Mrs. Tandy said, "I've never been in a rain this hard, nor a wind this wild. I hope we have a good driver."

Glen Taylor walked over to her and said, "He's ready to start. Why don't I sit down here next to you, Mrs. Tandy?

"Then I'll be able to help you guys if you need me."

Mrs. Tandy smiled and said, "Please, just call me Becky."

Sammy poked Bill. He whispered, "Why didn't he sit in the empty seat ACROSS from her? He'd have more room. Looks to me like Mrs. T.'s got a brand new boyfriend!"

He turned around to look at them,

16

and giggled.

Glen smiled his wide, easy smile.

He said, "What's wrong, Sammy? Am I sitting next to your lady love? I'm sorry, I am over-come by her beauty. May I kiss your hand, madam?"

He grabbed hold of her hand and lifted it toward his lips.

But at the last minute, he turned her hand over, so his was on top. Then SMACK! He gave his own hand a loud kiss.

He grinned a silly grin and said, "Um! I taste very good!"

He licked the top of his hand as if he were a juicy-tongued dog.

Mrs. Tandy and the rest began to giggle.

In a voice like a king's, Glen said, "What? My subjects are laughing at their Royal Highness? I won't have it!"

17

He tapped Sammy on top of his head with a rolled-up newspaper.

Sammy giggled even harder.

The bus rolled slowly out of the Nadi airport. It drove along fields almost hidden by rain.

Glen pulled a brown paper bag out of his roomy jacket pocket.

He said, "This bag is full of little bags of peanuts.

"The plane's crew discovered I was a king. So they gave me all the peanuts left over from the trip."

He handed a little bag to each of the five Woodlanders.

He opened one himself.

He looked hard at Sammy. He said, "These are not FLYING peanuts, young man, like the ones YOU had on the plane."

Then he said, "Oops! I must have

been wrong. These peanuts DO fly! One flew into your ear!"

He reached forward. He picked a peanut out of Sammy's ear.

Then he got another one off of Bill's nose.

Then he reached across and up the aisle to Kathy's shoulder. He held up his hand. He had another!

Sammy's mouth fell open. "How do you do that? Show me how! You're not

a king, really ... ARE YOU?"

Glen looked very serious. He said, "Oh, dear. I hope the driver didn't lose any of our bags. I left my crown in my carry-on."

Sammy said, "CROWN? Come on! What are you really? A magician?"

Glen shook his head. He said, "All right, you've found me out. I give up. I'm not a king. I'm something ten times more important."

Dave said, "What's that?"

Glen spread his arms wide, like an actor. He said, "I am a teacher."

Sammy moaned. "A teacher? You're a teacher?

"Will we have to keep quiet this whole trip?

"Some vacation!"

Chapter 3:
Mud Slides!

Glen laughed. He said, "Boy, do you have me figured wrong!"

Sammy said, "Well, what do you teach? Acting?"

Glen said, "No, I'm an art teacher. But acting is my hobby."

Bill looked worried.

Suddenly he said, "Look at that! Orange slime! Coming our way!"

Everybody looked to the left, where he was pointing. The rain had let up for a minute again. They saw a huge slab of runny orange mud, about three blocks wide.

It seemed to have poured down from the hills, like a river, almost to the road.

Kathy said, "Weird! There isn't a single thing growing out of it!"

Dave said, "It's a mud slide! It must have knocked down everything in its path!"

All of a sudden they heard a hiss, coming from right behind Mrs. Tandy and Glen.

It was Blossom Babberton.

She said, "Mud slides! How foolish! It's just an open field.

"They didn't show any mud slides in the travel folder. I'm sure there aren't any in Fiji!"

Glen turned and said, "Would you care to make a little bet on that?"

Mrs. Babberton glared at him, but stopped talking.

The rain fell even harder and blocked their view. It seemed to be falling not in drops, but in sheets.

The bus inched along through the raging storm.

Mrs. Babberton tapped Glen on the shoulder.

In a loud voice she said, "Have the boys take a message to the driver. Tell him to put on speed. He's far too slow.

"I want to be in Suva in time for dinner. The hotel expects us. Make those boys get up and give him my message."

Sammy glared at her.

He looked as mad as a tiger.

His hair stuck straight up like bristles on a hairbrush.

He had been listening to her blab for

the whole trip. In fact, he secretly called her POSSUM BLABBER-TONGUE instead of Blossom Babberton.

He wanted to tell her off!

But Bill poked him hard.

Sammy whispered, "All right, all right. I'll be polite. But Possum Blabber-tongue is the dumbest person I know ... even counting YOU, Poison-Poke!"

But Glen answered Mrs. Babberton for them all.

He twisted around to face her. He lifted his head high in the air.

He spread his long arms out wide ... so wide his bony wrists stuck out of his sleeves.

In his most kingly voice he said, "Madam, we are not message boys.

"And we certainly don't want the driver to speed along a slippery road in a hurricane.

"But perhaps he'd stop the bus and let you get off. You could wait by the side of the road for another bus ... perhaps one that went faster."

Mrs. Babberton just kept glaring at Glen.

Just then Dave said, "Look to the right, guys! The rain's letting up a little! You can see part of the ocean! Look at the color!"

The ocean was an angry, blue-black color.

But running into it along the shore were floods of orange earth, pouring into the sea.

Then the wind and rain started up even harder.

Mrs. Tandy said, "My, it doesn't sound like a million tapping fingers anymore. It sounds like a million flying stones ... the wind's blowing the rain so hard.

"It's the worst storm I've EVER seen ... and we had some knock-out storms where I grew up.

"We should be ready for any emergency. I think there's real danger!"

Mrs. Babberton put on her most sour look.

She said, "Well, I, for one, am a woman who doesn't know the MEANING of the word FEAR!"

Just then the bus swayed to the right, toward the ocean side of the road. For a moment it seemed almost as if it would tip into the orange flood.

Blossom Babberton SCREAMED! LOUD!

Dave began to slide off his seat!

Bill, Sammy, Kathy, Glen, and Mrs. Tandy were ready. They grabbed him and kept him from falling.

Sammy groaned. "When do we get to the things that were in the travel folder

... like sunny beaches ... and shells ... and rare animals ... and all that?"

Bill whispered, "Right now. There's a rare animal."

He pointed at Blossom Babberton.

She was lying against the bus window, eyes shut, mouth open.

The woman who didn't know the MEANING of the word FEAR ... had fainted!

Chapter 4:
An Orange Hug

The Woodlanders helped Mrs. Babberton lie down on the bus seat.

Kathy said, "There's a big bump on the back of her head.

"She must have hit the bottom edge of the window frame."

They washed her face with cool rain water.

Kathy patted her cheeks until she snapped out of it.

Mrs. Babberton opened her eyes and said, "What are you doing! Stop hitting me, young lady! Don't think I won't report this rudeness to the museum!"

Kathy said, "Don't you remember? We almost went off the road in the rain. You got scared and fainted."

Mrs. Babberton said, "Don't be foolish. I was just taking a little nap. Now leave me alone!"

The bus crept slowly along.

The driver sat at the very edge of his seat, trying to see better.

He turned his radio up louder so the passengers could all hear.

The voice said, " ... mud slides have covered a pig farm. All the pens are gone, and the animals are dead.

"The owner has run with his family to higher ground. He says they can never build the farm there again."

Sammy said, "Poor guy. I wish I could help him."

The radio voice went on. "Five people have been washed away by floodwaters. Four have been buried by mud slides.

31

"Water pumping stations are flooded. The water supply is ruined in many cities.

"Tank trucks carrying safe water are trying to reach the smaller towns. All drinking water must be boiled."

Kathy was looking at a map as she listened.

She said, "Look, there are two rivers between us and Suva. I wonder if they'll give us trouble."

At that very moment the radio voice said, "Rivers are flowing up over their banks. Some are six meters over their usual levels."

Dave said, "Six meters? A meter's a little longer than a yard! That means those rivers are eighteen FEET higher than usual!"

The radio continued, "Thousands of people have left their homes.

"Others are still living in their flooded

houses. They are moving through water up to their hips."

Sammy said, "Can't we do something to help them?"

Mrs. Babberton said, "Don't be silly. What could YOU do? You're just a child. Anyway, WE are the ones who need help!"

The bus driver called, "Look ahead!"

A road worker was waving at the driver and pointing about forty feet ahead to a smaller bus.

The driver turned around and said, "That little bus is stuck in the mud.

"They want to know if we can lend a hand and push it out. It will mean standing in deep, muddy water."

When everyone said they would help, Kathy shot a glance at Dave.

Dave said, "This is something I can't help with, but I'll watch from here."

One by one, everyone stepped out barefoot into the muddy, orange water ... except Mrs. Babberton.

The crowd splashed over to the little bus. They began to push.

Slowly, slowly, the bus moved back onto the road.

Everybody cheered and waved, but they were dripping with orange water!

Sammy grinned and said, "This isn't quite what I had in mind when I said I wanted to go swimming!"

They all piled back on the tour bus.

Mrs. Babberton said, "Look at you! You all look disGUSTing!"

Suddenly Glen put both arms forward. He ran to Mrs. Babberton and sat down.

He exclaimed, "And YOU kept so clean, my sweet woman!"

To everyone's surprise, he gave her a big hug.

Then he stood up.

Mrs. Babberton was covered with orange mud water!

Glen jumped back. He said, "Oh, no! Now YOU'RE disgusting, too!

"But don't worry. It will give me great happiness to have your dress cleaned. In fact, I'll save the cleaning bill forever!"

Finally their driver announced, "We are coming to a town we must pass to get to Suva. The ocean road is too low, and

35

will be flooded. We have to take the higher back road."

He turned left up a little jungle road.

Then he started downhill, until suddenly the bus stopped.

They all looked out the front window again.

The road had disappeared into a huge rushing flood of orange water.

And the water had ROOFtops sticking out of it!

Chapter 5:
Where Will We Sleep?

They saw another man waving from the side of the road!

The driver got out to talk to him.

The man told him that most of the

town was underwater.

There was no way to get through it to the hotel in Suva.

They had to turn back.

Mrs. Babberton said, "I INSIST that you get us to our Suva hotel!"

The driver said, "Well, you can insist all you want. But there's only one way you could get to Suva now ... swim there!"

Mrs. Babberton said, "You better find us another hotel, then. And get moving!"

The bus driver spoke to the group in a pleasant voice, "We did pass one hotel ... you can help me look for it on the right."

But when they found it, the lights were all off.

Bill said, "Sammy and I can run in and see if they can put us up!"

The boys dashed into the hotel.

Sammy said, "Whoa! What's going on here! Look at this!"

They were standing in the dark in water that came up to their ankles.

Bill said, "Hello! Anybody there?"

A faint voice answered, "I'm coming!"

A man splashed out of a black hall into the dark lobby. He was wearing a bathing suit. His face broke into a friendly smile when he saw the boys.

He said, "It's nice to see other human beings. Everyone but me is gone. The hotel is closed. I've just finished locking up for the owners.

"Now I have to get to my home, up the road toward Nadi."

Bill said, "Maybe you can ride with us! Come on!"

They ran to the bus.

Blossom Babberton said, "He's not part of our group. He shouldn't ride without paying."

But everyone else invited him to take a seat.

After they dropped him off, they drove and drove through the rain.

By now Sammy was really worried. He asked Bill, "What will we do if we don't find a place? Where will we sleep?"

Bill said, "It's OK, Sammy. We can

always sleep on the bus."

Just then the driver said, "Here's a place I know can take us."

On the right, the high side of the road, stood a modern motel.

Mrs. Tandy said, "But the sign hanging in the window says FULL."

The driver stood up and said, "Don't worry about that. I know something you don't!"

He jumped off the bus and ran inside.

In a few minutes he raced back waving a bunch of keys.

He yelled, "Follow me! Bring your things!"

Mrs. Babberton said, "He must be out of his mind. He's running into the jungle. I'm not following him in there!"

But the others got off the bus and headed into the wet, dark trees. So in a minute, Mrs. Babberton followed, too.

They all hurried down a thin path that ended in a clearing. There stood three big, beautiful houses.

The driver said, "Now first I have to tell you, you won't like the smell. But you'll get used to it. And you know the saying, 'Any port in a storm.'"

He chose a key and un-locked the first house.

Everyone hurried in after him, happy to be safe.

Then they smelled it.

"P-U!"

"Stink-o!"

"Hold your nose!"

"This must be a dump!"

"Turn on the lights!"

The lights went on.

Dave said, "Wow! Take a look at this place! It's beautiful!"

They were standing in a room as tall as the inside of a barn.

It was all white, with brown ceiling beams.

Couches and tables and chairs made the room look inviting.

Outside the high windows, shining jungle leaves danced in the storm.

The bus driver explained, "These houses are what's left of an old hotel.

"Two years ago new owners bought the land. They built a new motel, closer to the road.

43

"They added a store and a restaurant.

"They closed these houses and never used them again.

"There are four bedrooms and two bathrooms in each house. There are two beds in each bedroom. Make yourselves at home!"

Mrs. Babberton stamped her foot. "I could never feel at home in this terrible place! The smell is disGUSTing! I want a modern motel room!

"I deMAND to see the manager."

The driver said, "He's in the store down near the road.

"You'll have to go back through the jungle to talk to him. But you'll find that all his motel rooms are full."

Mrs. Babberton growled, "Well, then, at least take me to one of the OTHER buildings."

She looked hard at the Woodlanders

and Glen. "I will not stay in the same building with CERTAIN PEOPLE."

Then she marched out into the rain. The driver took her and some of the others to the other two houses.

In fifteen minutes everyone was settled in.

But Sammy felt gloomy.

He said, "What if the rain doesn't ever stop? Maybe I'll NEVER get to use my swim fins. A trip like this can sure disappoint a person."

Kathy said, "Then let's do something about it!

"Mom used to say that when it's raining, you have to make your own sunshine. And I think I have a great idea for how to do it!"

Chapter 6:
The Costume Party

Sammy said, "What's your idea, Kathy?
I'll tell you if it's great or not!"

Kathy said, "Let's have a costume
party at dinner!"

Sammy rolled his eyes. "It's great, except for one thing. No costumes."

Kathy said, "But we can make some. From stuff around here. From things in our suitcases!"

Sammy nodded. "OK, OK, I get it. Now that I think of it, I even know what I'm going to wear. But I'm not telling. It's a surprise!

"I'll run over to the other houses and tell them about the party."

Bill said, "I'll tell everyone here!"

Mrs. Tandy said, "I love to make costumes. But first, before I forget, I'm going to the motel store. I'm all out of toothpaste."

Kathy said, "I'll go with you."

They came running back through the rain with toothpaste ... and two big pieces of bright-flowered cloth.

Kathy flashed the cloth around in the

air. "We are going to wear these! The shopkeeper showed us how to wrap the cloth around our bodies the Fiji way!"

Dave said, "Well, I'm using the purple towel for a royal cape. And this blue one for a turban. I'm going as a prince!"

He wrapped the blue towel around his head. He put on the purple cape.

Bill said, "That's good. But I couldn't think of anything for me."

Sammy said, "This looks like a job for SUPER-SAM! I'll save you!"

He began scratching through Bill's suitcase like a dog digging out a rabbit hole.

He said, "Quick, guys! Go through everything you own!"

But all they came up with were sweaters and jeans and running pants and shirts.

Sammy wouldn't give up. He said, "I know! Bill could wear socks on his hands, like paws."

Bill said, "PAWS! I could go as a monster!"

Mrs. Tandy reached for her bag. She said, "I have blue and green and black eye make-up, and lip stick. We can give you a monster face."

Sammy said, "I've got it, Bill! Put on your big sweatshirt. We can stuff it until you're all lumpy. Lumpy monsters are the best."

So they fastened a belt around Bill's sweatshirt. They stuffed clothes inside it, around his body, arms, and legs.

Kathy opened the eye make-up. She gave him a blue face and black whiskers.

Mrs. Tandy said, "How about this for a monster hat?" She dumped out her purse and put it upside-down on Bill's head.

She exclaimed, "You're perfect, Bill! Now the only one who doesn't have a costume is you, Sammy. Just what did you have in mind?"

Sammy said, "First make my face greenish, Mrs. T. And draw my mouth so wide it touches my ears, like a frog's. Then I'll show you my costume."

In a few minutes he came flip-flapping out of his room.

He had on his fins and a bright green running suit.

He wore his diving goggles.

He said, "See, I got to wear my swim fins after all. I'm a frog!"

He hopped around the living room and they all cheered.

Then in walked the tour leader, Tina Chow. She wore her regular clothes, but back to front and inside out. They clapped and she took a bow.

Next came the people from another bedroom. The woman was dressed in her husband's white pajamas. She carried a thermometer.

"I'm a doctor," she said. "And Henry's my patient!"

Her husband was wearing a bathrobe and slippers. He had bandages stuck all over his face and hands.

Everyone clapped again.

Suddenly Glen Taylor leaped into the living room.

He announced, "I'm a beautiful Fiji woman!"

He was dressed in bright Fiji cloth. He had huge red flowers in his hair, stuck into the sweatband.

He had borrowed some large earrings and bracelets.

He began singing a made-up Fiji song. He started dancing a wild dance, with his huge bare toes sticking straight up, and his bony elbows sticking out.

Sammy giggled. "Beautiful WOMAN? You look more like a giant grasshopper having a fit!"

Glen raised his arms high over his head like a ballet dancer.

Then he JUMPED at Sammy. He pulled the bottom of Sammy's sweatshirt up over his head and held it there.

He said, "We beautiful Fiji women know an insult when we hear one."

Sammy laughed and tried to fight his way out.

He called from inside his sweat shirt, "You'd probably look a lot more beautiful if you didn't have a mustache!"

Glen said, "Who needs advice from a frog? Let's go eat."

The other people at the restaurant clapped as they entered.

But all through dinner everyone talked about the rain.

At last Sammy said, "I'm tired of all this rain talk. Why don't we DO something about it?"

Bill asked, "Like what?"

Sammy said, "Well, you've heard of rain dances ... we could do an UN-RAIN dance!"

He began chanting, "It's raining, it's pouring. The old man is snoring.

"Rain, rain, go away. Come again some other day. Little children want to play. Rain, rain, go away."

Bill said, "Shh ... Sammy, you'll bother the other people."

But smiling strangers at the other

tables had begun clapping in time to Sammy's chant. Pretty soon everyone in the room was clapping and chanting.

Then Glen jumped up and started to march around the restaurant in time to the chant.

One by one the Woodlanders got up and followed him ...

and so did the museum group

and the other diners

and the waiters and waitresses

... and pretty soon everyone was up and laughing, except, of course, Blossom Babberton.

Finally they were all worn-out. They dropped into their chairs.

Dave said, "I guess we should get to bed now.

"Tomorrow we have to try again to get to Suva. I wonder if we ever WILL get there?"

Chapter 7: Mrs. Babberton Turns Purple

It was morning.

Sammy jumped out of bed and ran to the window.

The sun was shining through the

jungle leaves. The rain had stopped!

He ran back to the bed and pulled the covers off of Bill.

He said, "Wake up! Wake up! It stopped raining! The sun's out!"

He ducked the pillow Bill threw at him.

Then they heard a loud pounding on the door.

Tina Chow stuck her head into their room.

She called, "Pack up, everybody! Now's our chance to try to get to Suva!

"Let everybody know we will start at ten o'clock. Breakfast is as soon as you're ready!"

They all got dressed quickly.

Everybody met in the living room.

Sammy said, "SEE? My un-rain dance stopped the rain! Now I'm going to figure out my next plan!

"I'm going to earn some money to give to the Fiji Red Cross! I heard on the bus radio that they're helping people who've been flooded out!"

Bill smiled. "Great! If you figure out how, I'll help you do it."

Kathy said, "I'll help, too!"

Dave said, "Count me in."

Mrs. Tandy added, "Me, too!"

They boarded the bus. As it crawled slowly along, they saw there was still a lot of water on the road.

People were standing along the way to show where the sides had washed out.

But by noon they reached the river town that had been underwater. The roads were open now!

Slowly, slowly, they crawled along to Suva.

At 3:00 the driver finally stopped in front of their hotel.

A cheer went up from their bus.

Men in skirts and jackets helped them carry in their bags.

Sammy hit Bill on the arm and said, "For once you weren't kidding me. Men really DO wear skirts here. And they look great!"

Mrs. Babberton got off the bus.

She marched up to Mrs. Tandy. She said, "At last I am in a place where I will get the treatment I SHOULD get!"

She marched up to the hotel desk. She cut in front of the people already there. She said, "Clerk, I can't wait. I have to get to my room right away.

"I'm feeling quite sick and tired. I have had a very bad time.

"I INSIST you give me my key this minute."

To get rid of her, the clerk gave her a room key.

But after she got into her room she was in for a big surprise.

The manager knocked on every door. He called the guests to come into the hall. Then he stood in front of stacks of big, new plastic pails.

He said, "I'm sorry to tell you this. The Suva water station has broken down.

"You can only get a drip of water from your faucets. But we had some water trucked in.

61

"We will boil it and use it to drink, and for cooking. But you must not drink water dripping from the faucets.

"It isn't boiled and could make you very sick."

Sammy clapped. "Hooray! I won't have to brush my teeth for two days!"

The manager said, "Oh, you'll be able to brush your teeth, all right. Use the sugar-free pop from your room refrigerator."

Sammy said, "Well, at least I'll be able to snorkel in your pool. I'm going in right now for a swim."

The manager said, "I'm afraid not, my boy.

"The floodwaters have washed into it, too. It's full of germs. You can't risk swimming in it."

He pointed to his stack of buckets and said, "But the water from it will be used ... for something else.

"I'm giving each room one of these plastic pails. To flush your toilets, you'll have to pour a pail of water into them.

"You will have to go down to the swimming pool to fill your pails."

Mrs. Babberton turned bright red. She screamed, "You stupid man!

"Do you think I'm going up and down a flight of steps every time I want to flush the toilet? In the middle of the night? In slippers and a nightgown?"

The manager said, "You can wear whatever you like when you do it, madam ... but you must understand this is an emergency. We have over three hundred guests.

"Half our workers can't get here. They're stuck in flooded homes."

Now Mrs. Babberton turned as purple as a beet. She hissed, "Well, I am NOT going to carry my own water!

"And the OTHER guests won't want to, either!"

Sammy ran up to her and grabbed her hand. He said, "Mrs. Babberton, thank you. You just gave me a great idea! Thanks a lot!"

She shook her fingers loose, as if Sammy were a disgusting animal.

She went into her room and slammed the door.

But Sammy was grinning from ear to ear.

Chapter 8:
The Water Crew

Sammy was thrilled!

He said, "Wait till I tell you my great idea, guys!"

But before he could say any more,

Tina Chow spoke up.

She said, "Well, at least we GOT here. We are a day late, but we do have part of the afternoon left.

"We can go to the Suva Museum as we planned.

"And tomorrow we can visit the fruit market. And re-visit the museum. And catch some sun!

"We don't have to head back to Nadi till late afternoon tomorrow."

So they all got on the bus to go to the Suva Museum.

Bill said, "Look at all this sun!"

Sammy grinned and said, "See how good my un-rain dance was?"

But an hour later they were racing out of the museum through another wild storm.

Bill, Sammy, and Glen Taylor carried Dave aboard the bus.

Kathy and Mrs. Tandy were right behind them.

Everyone was soaking wet.

Mrs. Tandy pushed Sammy's wet hair out of his eyes. She said, "So much for your un-rain dance, honey.

"I'm sorry about your snorkeling, but I don't think it's going to happen on this trip!"

Sammy surprised them all.

He said, "It's OK. Don't worry. We are going to be busy all night tonight … I guess I'd be too tired to go snorkeling tomorrow, anyway."

Bill said, "What do you mean, we are going to be busy all night?"

Sammy said, "I'll show you my secret plan after dinner."

They ate. Then Sammy found the hotel manager. He borrowed a black marker and a big sheet of paper from him.   In a few minutes he had finished his sign.

He hung it on the door of the room he and Bill and Dave were using.

The   sign   didn't   say   THE WOODLANDERS.

Instead it said:

The Water Crew
Day and Night
We Carry Pails
Knock on this Door
for Water from the Pool
Brought to Your Room
Cost: a Donation to the
Fiji Red Cross

Less than one minute later they heard a knock on the door.

It was an older man with a pail. He had been going for water himself until he saw the sign.

He said, "Was I glad to see that! A big pail of water is HEAVY!"

Sammy nodded. "I know. My teacher says, 'A pint's a pound, the whole world round.' It's only ABOUT a pound, not a pound exactly.

"But these pails can hold three gallons of water.

"And there are four quarts in every gallon.

"That's twelve quarts.

"And there are two pints in every quart.

"So that's twenty-four pints.

"And do you know about how many pounds that is? It's—"

The man stopped him. "Yes, yes, you can spare me the math lesson.

"Just bring me up a pail of water, Room 238 ... and here's money for the Red Cross."

So Sammy said, "Oh, yes, SIR, right AWAY, sir!"

He picked up the man's pail.

He trotted down the steps. A tall man in a gray jacket and a blue skirt opened the door to the outside pool.

Another hotel worker, dressed the same way, stood next to the pool.

He took the pail from Sammy, and dipped up water for him.

Sammy ran back inside, and met Kathy coming down with another pail.

And Mrs. Tandy was following with another one!

Then Bill came along. He was carrying TWO pails.

Back at the room, Dave was sitting outside the door.

He had a little notebook.

He was writing numbers in it when Sammy came back up.

Dave said, "I'm keeping track of what people donate.

"So far they've given everything from a one-dollar bill to much more.

"Of course, I'm not really sure how much more ... there's money from all over the world in here!"

Sammy said, "Wow! Where are you keeping it?"

Dave pointed to a pail next to his wheelchair.

The bottom was already covered with bills and coins.

By then two women had come along with their pails.

One of them put a whole handful of bills into the money pail.

The other woman was Blossom Babberton.

She said, "If you had any good manners at all, you children would be doing this for free."

She made a sour face.

She fished out nine pennies from her purse and handed them to Dave.

Dave just said, "Thanks for your donation, Mrs. Babberton."

But he lifted the money pail to his

lap. He wanted her to see how much was in there.

Then he winked a giant wink at Sammy, and Sammy trotted off to get the two women their water.

All night long the Woodlanders carried pails of water.

By 6:00 in the morning they had a whole bucket jammed full of money.

Mrs. Tandy's eyelids were drooping. She said, "I feel like an all-night rider for the old Pony Express. People can carry their own water from now on.

"Let's go to bed!"

Sammy yawned. "Let's just skip the museum.

"And the market.

"And the beach."

Kathy said, "Yep. Let's just skip into bed."

Sammy said, "But first, let's get this

money to the Red Cross office!"

But just then Tina Chow called the museum group into the hall—even the ones who had been sleeping!

She said, "Bad luck, folks. I'm dropping all our plans for the day.

"We've got a new emergency."

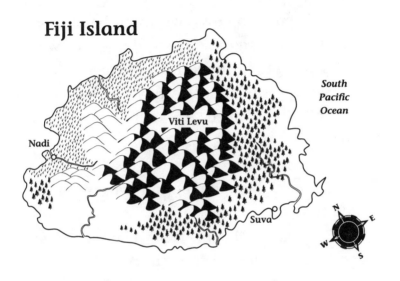

Fiji Island

South Pacific Ocean

Viti Levu

Nadi

Suva

Chapter 9:
The Race with the River

Kathy said, "What's wrong?"

Tina said, "The weather forecast is terrible. More rain is due.

"We have to head back to the Nadi

airport right now! No waiting until afternoon.

"We have to cross two rivers before the road floods again. If we don't, we will miss our plane home tonight."

Sammy said, "So we have to wait until Nadi to turn in our Red Cross money?"

Tina nodded.

By now Mrs. Babberton was mad ... really mad.

She said, "I am NOT leaving Suva without seeing the fruit market.

"And I INSIST we go to the beach!

"Why, the weather looks perfectly beautiful!"

Sammy whispered to Bill, "There goes old Possum Blabber-tongue again."

But Tina only said, "I'm sorry. The bus is leaving in half an hour."

Half-asleep, the Woodlanders packed.

They dragged out to the bus with their suitcases and climbed aboard.

They fell asleep in the bright sunlight.

Hours later, rain pouring down, something woke them.

It was the bus, shaking like a baby's rattle, coming to a stop.

The driver announced, "We have a flat tire."

Tina said, "OK, everybody! Please get off the bus so we can fix this quickly and get across those rivers!"

Mrs. Babberton said, "I'll get soaked out there in the rain. I'm not getting off!"

So the others got off. She stayed inside and fell asleep a few minutes later.

Bill said to the driver, "Sammy and I will work the jack for you."

Dave said, "Hand me the lugs as you take them off. I'll keep them in the hubcap so they don't get lost."

The driver un-screwed the bolts that held the wheel. He handed them to Dave.

Then he said, "Start jacking up the bus, boys! And don't jiggle it, anyone ... the jack might slip on all these wet rocks!"

Finally the flat tire was lifted off the road.

But at that moment Mrs. Babberton woke up and looked around her.

She found the bus door closed.

She felt TRAPPED.

She banged on the door and jumped up and down on the step.

The bus began to shake.

The driver yelled to her to stop.

But she took a running jump from near the driver's seat. She RAMMED against the door.

The bus shook. The jack slipped.

Dave yelled, "Get back from the bus!"

Bill grabbed Sammy and they fell back off the road.

Mrs. Tandy and Kathy pulled Glen away from the bus.

The bus crashed down.

When Dave looked around, he saw:

Glen Taylor sitting on Mrs. Tandy's lap.

Glen's feet lying across Kathy.

Bill in the mud with Sammy on his stomach.

The bus driver's head resting on Sammy's feet.

But they were all safe.

The others ran up and helped them up.

Now THEY were all muddy, too.

The bus driver opened the bus door for Mrs. Babberton.

She stepped out. She looked around

at the crowd and said, "Well! Here you are, playing in the mud again like pigs!

"I'm going to report you all to the museum! You will never go on a trip with Blossom Babberton, EVER AGAIN!"

Mrs. Tandy said, "You can say that again!"

Bill said, "Come on, Sammy. We've got to change that tire and cross those rivers, or it'll be too late."

Chapter 10: Stuck!

They worked fast.

They got the spare tire on.

Finally, the bus moved slowly toward the high part of town.

They crossed the bridge over the rushing river!

Sammy said, "We did it! One down, one to go! We can get this money to the Red Cross today after all!"

Workers on the other side told them not to take the high road this time. It was covered by a mud slide.

So the bus driver headed toward the ocean instead.

The road to the ocean ran quite close to the swollen river.

Sammy said, "There's water all over this road! I hate this! How does the driver even know where the road is?"

Bill said, "It's OK, Sammy. I bet he's driven this way a million times."

Just as Bill said that, the bus dipped down ... and then rose up again.

They heard the motor stop ... and start again ... and stop.

Then the bus rolled to a dead standstill.

The driver tried to start it a few times. Then he said, "Well, folks, there's good news and bad news.

"First the good news. We crossed this river just in time!"

Kathy said, "What's the bad news?"

The driver answered, "Here it is. The road back there had a deep hole in it, under the water. I couldn't see it, so we dipped down into it.

"The spark plugs got wet. We are stuck here until they dry out."

Everybody groaned, except for Mrs. Babberton ... who threw a fit.

Sammy couldn't stand it.

He glared at Mrs. Babberton.

Bill took one look at him and said, "Hey, since we are just stuck here, let's play a game!"

Kathy said, "How about some animal game?"

Glen said, "Let's list the strangest animals we know.

"And I'll give a prize for the best one. I'll start ... I went to Australia last year and saw some DOOZIES!"

Sammy asked, "What animal is that? I've never heard of a doozy."

Glen laughed. He said, "A doozy isn't an animal! Doozy just means something wonderful.

"The best animal I saw in Australia was a duck-billed platypus."

Sammy said, "Really? A duck-billed platypus? I love the name. What's it like? Would it make a good pet?"

Glen said, "It's cute and furry, with a bill like a duck's. But it WOULDN'T make a good pet. The male has poison glands in its hind claws!"

Sammy said, "Just a minute. It's got a bill like a duck's AND fur? Then is it a bird or a mammal?"

Glen said, "Well, it gives milk like a mammal. But it lays eggs like a bird. It's a monotreme." He said the word like this: MON-uh-treem.

"Now, how about you, Dave? What's your strangest animal?"

Dave said, "I choose the rock hyrax." He said it like this: HIGH-racks.

"I saw it in a book about African animals.

"It sort of looked to me like a huge groundhog.

"The funny part is, its closest relative is the elephant.

"And it's the only animal with hooves that climbs trees all the time!"

Sammy said, "Now it's my turn!"

He thought for a minute. Then he said, "Well, how about this?

"In science class we read about this animal that lives in about every temperature ... even freezing ... even where it's too hot for other animals."

Bill said, "I bet it's a fox. I was just reading about foxes!"

Sammy rolled his eyes. "Boy, are you far off!

"Here's a hint. My animal can change from one shape to another ... like a blob of runny jelly ... like a one-celled animal ... like an amoeba!" He said the word like this: uh-ME-buh.

Kathy said, "Is this a science-fiction animal?"

Sammy shook his head. "Nope. It changes shape like an amoeba, because it IS an amoeba! That's my animal!

"Hah! Gotcha!"

Bill said, "No fair! You can't even see an amoeba without a microscope!"

Sammy stuck out his tongue and said, "No one ever said you had to be able to see the animal without a microscope!

"We never even talked about a microscope. So I win."

Bill said, "You wish, pest. Wait till you hear about these frogs!"

Sammy laughed. "Bill's choosing FROGS.

"Bill, you're not going to win the prize

with stupid old FROGS."

Bill said, "STUPID! I read in a newspaper about some African frogs. They were HUGE! They weighed seven pounds each!"

Mrs. Tandy laughed. "Are you sure that wasn't a comic book you were reading?"

Bill said, "Yep. It's true. And those aren't even the BEST frogs. There are father frogs that raise their babies in their throats.

"And strawberry poison dart frogs that wrestle with each other.

"Anyway, it's your turn, Kathy."

But at that moment the bus driver called, "I think we can get going in just a few minutes!"

Chapter 11: Saved!

The driver said, "The spark plugs must be nearly dry by now."

Dave said, "At least the rain has stopped down here. But it must still be raining up in the hills.

"See? The river's still flooded. Look at it go!"

The driver said, "Maybe you'd like to go outside and get a better look.

"Last chance to move around before we get to Nadi!"

Most of the passengers got off.

The Woodlanders and Glen lowered Dave out of the bus.

They looked across the road at the river roaring alongside it.

Dave said, "Let's go closer. But not too close to the edge."

Sammy led the way with big frog hops, saying, "B-r-u-u-p! B-r-u-u-p!" deep in his throat.

Bill said, "Was that a burp?"

Sammy shouted, "No! I'm a HUGE African frog!"

They stood watching the river.

All sorts of things had been washed into it by the storm.

Branches of trees bobbed and rushed toward the ocean.

A wooden door sailed past them.

Bill said, "Some of our Red Cross money might help re-build houses. Maybe even the house that door came from."

A dead cow floated along.

Then a giant leafy tree came into sight, twisting slowly around.

Sammy yelled, "Look! The whole trunk and branches and everything! It got pulled out, roots and all!"

The tree jammed against the land, just below where they were standing.

Its branches hit some thick bushes that grew there, and tangled with them. The trunk swung around.

It stuck almost straight out into the

fast-running water.

It bobbed up and down.

Mrs. Tandy pointed. "That tree won't stay tangled in the bushes very long. Look how the water keeps grabbing at it."

Suddenly Dave said, "Quick! Help me get to the edge!"

Kathy wheeled him closer.

Dave leaned toward the river.

He took a long look at the tree.

Then he placed his hands on the arms of his chair.

Before anyone could say anything, he gave a mighty push ... and threw himself forward out of his chair.

He shot over the edge of the riverbank and landed in the wild river.

Kathy screamed, "Dave!"

The next minute they saw him swimming, hard.

He couldn't move his legs, so his strong arms were all he could count on.

They watched him pull himself through the water, fighting with all his might.

Suddenly he stopped swimming.

He let the water carry him into the tree's branches.

Now the others saw why he had

pushed off into the river.

Bill yelled, "Hey! There's a little kid hanging on to that branch!"

Sammy said, "He's nearly drowning! The water keeps sucking him under! He's hardly hanging on!"

The child looked three or four years old.

They could see he was screaming, but they couldn't hear him.

The roaring river covered any other sounds.

Now Dave had hold of the boy. He lifted him with one arm. He wrapped his other arm tight around a branch.

Kathy yelled, "We've got to get them out, FAST! Before the tree breaks loose and they're washed into the ocean!"

Near the river, right near the edge, stood a strong, young tree.

Bill ran and hooked his arm around it.

Sammy grabbed Bill's free hand and said, "I'll go first!"

Bill said, "Kick off your shoes, and hang on tight!"

For once Sammy didn't argue.

Glen already had his shoes off. He said, "Hold me, Sammy."

Sammy took hold of Glen's hand, and Glen joined him in the river.

But even stretching out his long arms he couldn't reach Dave.

Mrs. Tandy had watched long enough. She shouted, "Here I come!"

Glen gave her his hand and she jumped into the water with him.

But she couldn't quite reach far enough to touch Dave.

Then Bill and Sammy pulled the others back to the riverbank.

Kathy was ready.

Mrs. Tandy took Kathy's hand, and they all rushed back in.

The water wasn't too cold, but it pounded hard and pushed them around.

Mrs. Tandy held on to Kathy for dear life. She pushed her out toward Dave.

The river pulled Kathy under. She kicked her way to the top again.

She gasped for air and grabbed for Dave, but missed.

She grabbed again, toward his arm that held on to the branch. This time she got hold of his wrist.

Dave let go of the branch and grabbed Kathy's wrist.

He still held the child above the water with his other arm.

The big tree began to jump like a bucking horse.

The other people had run up to help. They crowded around Bill.

Grabbing Sammy, they began to pull the human chain back to land.

They got Sammy up on shore, then Glen, then Mrs. Tandy, then Kathy.

Finally they pulled Dave and the child onto land.

One second later the big tree broke loose.

The wild river spun it around and swept it away to sea.

Chapter 12:
Here's the Money!

The Woodlanders, Glen, and the child were safe.

The child was coughing and spitting up river water.

He had leaves and bits of soft bark and sticks in his hair.

Some kind of black oil spotted his skin and clothes.

He was bleeding a little from a dozen scratches.

Kathy checked him over. She said, "There aren't any deep cuts, and nothing seems broken.

"I'll wash him off as soon as we get to some clean water."

Now the child was half-crying, half-choking, spitting out water.

After a minute he quieted down and took a good look around him.

He saw there wasn't a single person he knew!

He began crying again, louder! In fact, he was BAWLING!

He screamed, "Mama! Mama!"

Mrs. Tandy stretched out her arms.

She said, "Here, honey. We will find your mama. Don't cry."

But the sobbing child just hit her hands away.

He looked around the crowd again. Then he reached out both his thin little arms and cried, "Mama!"

Who was he reaching for? BLOSSOM BABBERTON!

Everyone gasped. They knew how she felt about children.

But the next minute she walked up to Dave. She said, "Give me that baby."

Then she took the wet, bleeding, oil-spotted child in her arms!

She hugged him against her clean dress.

She kissed his dirty cheeks.

She patted him on the back and began chanting a little song she made up as she went along:

103

"You're my baby bun-ny
You're my little hon-ey
You're my little fun-ny
You're my little son-ny."

Sammy blurted out, "HEY! I thought you HATED kids!"

Mrs. Babberton sniffed and said, "This is no KID!

"This is a BABY! And didn't you see? He CHOSE ME!"

Sammy whispered to Bill, "Man, I feel sorry for her own kids after they stopped being babies!"

Everyone helped Mrs. Babberton carry the child onto the bus. Glen wrapped them in his big terry-cloth bathrobe.

Then Sammy fished out a chocolate bar from his carry-on bag.

Bill said, "SAMMY! That's MY candy bar! I was looking for it!"

Sammy said, "Well, I found it in your shoe under your bed this morning. How was I supposed to know it was yours!"

He fed some to the little boy, and some to Dave. He said, "After all, you two were in the river the longest. You need this to help you warm up."

He tried to give Mrs. Babberton a piece, but she said, "Get that away from me! Your hands are dirty!"

She hugged the little boy close to her chest.

In a while they were both asleep.

The bus made it past the second river ... with no problem ... and headed for the airport.

Even before they got there, they found out who the child was.

The bus radio brought this news:

"Emergency alert! A woman reports her three-year-old son is missing! She saw him climbing a huge tree when a flash flood hit her farm.

"The tree was up-rooted by the force of the water.

"Police fear the child is dead, but ask everyone to be on the lookout for him."

Finally, the museum group arrived at the airport in Nadi!

The whole crowd cheered for the bus driver.

The Woodlanders brought Mrs. Babberton and the child to a police officer right away.

When they told him about the rescue, he thanked them and said, "It's a miracle this baby's alive!

"Here, I'll take him off your hands till we find his folks."

He reached for the child, but the little boy screamed. He stuck like glue to Mrs. Babberton.

Mrs. Babberton said to the police officer, "He doesn't want to go with you, young man. He wants to stay with the one he likes. ME!"

So the officer said, "Then will you kind people keep him for a while in the waiting room? I'll let you know when someone comes for him."

He led them to a private airport bathroom.

Kathy washed the child's scratches.

Then she opened her first aid kit.

She put medicine and bandages on his worst cuts.

Sammy and Bill worked at getting the black oil out of his hair.

Dave dressed him in one of Kathy's clean T-shirts.

Mrs. Tandy washed his dirty clothes in the sink.

Then Sammy picked up the pail of money. He hurried off to the Red Cross desk.

Sammy held the pail in the air and said, "This is for you! It's from the Woodland family!"

The woman behind the counter joked, "A water pail? Don't tell me you're giving us WATER. That's the LAST thing we need!"

She leaned over the desk and looked into the big pail. Her eyes almost popped out of her head!

She said, "Why, it's just STUFFED with money! That's exactly what we DO need!

"We have tents with hundreds of families living in them.

"They need food, clothes, blankets, medicine ... almost everything!

"Where did you get all this?

"Wait a minute, don't tell me yet."

She turned and called to a woman standing nearby. "Come over here, Pat! You're a reporter, and this could be a good story for you!"

But at that moment they heard the loudspeaker: "Will the party that rescued the child from the river, please come to the information desk?"

Sammy blurted out, "I have to go find my family! Here's the money! If you want to talk, follow me!"

He rushed toward the information desk.

After him rushed the woman from the Red Cross.

And after her rushed the reporter with her camera!

Chapter 13:
The Strangest Animal

The whole museum group, all nineteen, were at the desk.

The child was still sticking to Mrs. Babberton like bark to a tree.

A big man was standing at the information desk with the police officer. He laughed when he saw the boy, and then began to cry.

He was the child's father.

The boy took one look at his dad.

He un-glued himself from Mrs. Babberton and grabbed his father.

He buried his head in his dad's shoulder.

Now he wouldn't even LOOK at Mrs. Babberton!

Bill saw the hurt look on her face and felt sorry for her.

He said, "Don't feel bad. He likes you. He's just glad to see his father again."

But Mrs. Babberton said, "That ungrateful little pig! And here I am with my dress a dirty mess!

"That's what you get for being nice to someone!"

Suddenly even Sammy felt sorry for Mrs. Babberton.

He thought of how un-happy she always made herself. She only saw the bad side of things.

He patted Mrs. Babberton on the arm, but she pushed his hand away.

He whispered to Bill, "I'm never going to call her Possum Blabber-tongue again. She just doesn't know how to be friends, that's all."

He patted her arm again. This time she didn't push him away.

The boy's father thanked them over and over.

The reporter asked about the river rescue. They told their story into her tape recorder.

They told how Mrs. Babberton took care of the child, too.

Then the reporter asked about the pail

113

full of money. The Woodlanders told her all about that.

The woman from the Red Cross said, "Their story is SO important to us. Could you put it on the front page?

"When people see it, I bet they'll want to raise money to help, too!"

Then the reporter took pictures.

In one, she had them all hold the pail handle with one hand.

And she had them hold up some money with the other.

She took pictures of the whole museum group.

And she took one of Dave holding the little boy. (He kicked Dave on the nose during that one.)

But Mrs. Babberton wouldn't pose for a picture. She said her dress was much too dirty.

At last the excitement was over. They still had an hour before the plane was supposed to take off.

Suddenly Sammy exclaimed, "Hey! We haven't finished our animal game yet! And nobody's won the prize!

"What IS the prize, anyway, Glen?"

Glen said, "My pocketknife from Hong Kong!"

He pulled a little knife from his pocket. It was shaped exactly like a fish.

Sammy said, "It's beautiful! Who gets it!"

Glen laughed. "Wait a minute, Sammy! Whoa! Becky and Kathy never got their turns."

Mrs. Tandy said, "All I thought of was a fish I read about. It spits out a shot of water.

"The water knocks bugs off of over-hanging leaves, and the fish eats them!"

Bill said, "Wow! What's yours, Kathy?"

Kathy smiled shyly and said, "I think I've got the strangest animal on earth.

"Some of these animals walk up-right, but this one rolls along.

116

"It's about the size of a large human.

"It eats what we eat.

"It's one of the smartest animals you'll ever meet.

"But it risks its life when it sees a person in trouble."

Sammy said, "I know! I've got it! It's a Saint Bernard dog!

"But ... that wouldn't explain the rolling-along part.

"I guess it can't be a Saint Bernard. OK, I give up. But this better be a real animal!"

Kathy nodded. "It is a real animal! It's a Dave Briggs!"

She turned bright red, and so did Dave!

Then Dave laughed, but Glen said, "Kathy wins the prize.

"Her animal IS the strangest! And everything she said about Dave is true!"

Glen handed Kathy the knife and bowed deeply. "You're the winner, Kathy, that's for sure."

But Kathy turned to Dave. She made a deep bow, too, still blushing.

She said, "I'm giving the prize to you, Dave. You're the one who put on the swimming show today.

"You earned a knife shaped like a fish!"

The museum group all began to clap (except for Mrs. Babberton, who was asleep, of course).

Then the other people in the airport looked toward Dave and clapped, too.

The loudspeaker boomed, "Time to board for Flight 118."

So the Woodlanders got on the plane.

They took off in the pouring rain ... talking and laughing ... eating more peanuts ... and ready for the next adventure.